Wild Water
MAGiC

Wild Water
MAGiC

by Lynne Jonell
illustrated by Brandon Dorman

A STEPPING STONE BOOK™
Random House 🏠 New York

To Marlene Glaus, my wonderful third grade
teacher! —L.J.

For our Molly-Bug —B.D.

Text copyright © 2014 by Lynne Jonell
Jacket art and interior illustrations copyright © 2014 by Brandon Dorman

All rights reserved. Published in the United States by Random House Children's
Books, a division of Random House LLC, a Penguin Random House Company,
New York.

Random House and the colophon are registered trademarks and A Stepping Stone
Book and the colophon are trademarks of Random House LLC.

Visit us on the Web!
SteppingStonesBooks.com
randomhouse.com/kids

Educators and librarians, for a variety of teaching tools,
visit us at RHTeachersLibrarians.com

Library of Congress Cataloging-in-Publication Data
Jonell, Lynne.
Wild water magic / by Lynne Jonell ; illustrated by Brandon Dorman.
p. cm. — (Magical mix-ups ; 4)
"A Stepping Stone Book."
Summary: "After Tate falls into a magic well in her backyard, she can read a book in
minutes. But she's strangely attracted to water of all sorts and can't always control her
magic." —Provided by publisher.
ISBN 978-0-375-87085-9 (trade) — ISBN 978-0-375-97085-6 (lib. bdg.) —
ISBN 978-0-307-97470-9 (ebook)
[1. Water—Fiction. 2. Learning—Fiction. 3. Magic—Fiction. 4. Brothers and sisters—
Fiction.] I. Dorman, Brandon, illustrator. II. Title.
PZ7.J675Wi 2014 [Fic]—dc23 2013036590

Printed in the United States of America
10 9 8 7 6 5 4 3 2 1

Contents

CHAPTER I

That's So Unfair!

Most people liked Tate Willow. They thought she was nice. They thought she was pretty. They thought she was smart.

Tate didn't think she was smart at all. School was harder for her than it was for other kids.

Sometimes letters and words got mixed up in her brain. Sometimes she forgot to do things in the right order. It took Tate twice as long as anyone else to finish her homework—but she tried to keep that a secret.

Last year, at her old school, she'd gotten some extra help with reading. And by the time school let out in June, she had improved. She was still not a fast reader, but her reading teacher said Tate remembered what she read better than anyone.

Finally! There was something she was good at!

So Tate had decided that when school started again in the fall, she would try out for the Book Quiz Team.

She liked the idea of sitting at a table with a buzzer in front of her and pressing it when she knew the answer. She liked the idea of making points for her team. She liked the idea of seeing her family in the audience. They'd be proud of her and clap for her. They'd say, "Tate's our reader!"

Tate had copied the list of books she would have to read during the summer. And by the first day at her new school, she had read every one.

Only now she wished she hadn't. What was the use? She would never make the Quiz Team. The handout she had gotten today made that very clear.

Tate stepped off the big yellow school bus. Her shoulders slumped. Her backpack dragged in the dust of the country road.

Abner, Derek, and Celia Willow leaped off the bus behind their sister and raced to the stone arch bridge. Every day after school, the four Willow children liked to drop sticks in the river below. Then they rushed to the other side of the bridge to see which stick came out first.

"Ready—set—" Abner began. Then he said, "Tate! Come on. We're waiting!"

"Go ahead without me," Tate called. She

walked slowly to the bridge and sat on its stone ledge. She didn't feel like playing. She just watched the river.

The river was usually a quiet, slow stream that curled around Hollowstone Hill like a sleepy blue snake. But now, after two weeks of rain, it was a muddy brown snake, wide awake and moving fast.

The sticks swirled and tumbled as they came out from under the bridge. One hit a rock with a sharp *crack*. Derek and Celia could not agree which stick had come out first, so they picked up new sticks and started over.

Abner sat down beside Tate. "What are you going to join at school this year?" he asked. "I'm going to be in the Science Club. We're building robots!"

Tate shoved her backpack a little with her toe. Of course Abner would be in the Science

Club. He had brains. He did his homework *three* times as fast as she did, and he was only one year older.

"I'm doing peewee football," Derek said. He stood on his hands in the middle of the bridge. "Maybe I'll do Scouts, too." He had found an old scouting handbook of his father's and had been trying to learn the different knots.

Tate's leg swung back and forth. *Bump–bump–bump* went her foot against her backpack. She could hardly do a cartwheel, and she had failed her last swimming test. But Derek was a star at every sport he tried. She supposed he would be good at tying knots, too. Why did things come so easily for everyone else?

Celia gave up on her stick and leaned against Abner's knee. "Miss Beeful put my picture of a dog up on the bulletin board. She says I should enter the art contest for my grade this year."

Celia sighed happily. "Miss Beeful says I take after my mother, because we're both talented artists."

Tate dangled her backpack by its strap and kicked it up in the air a little. Then she caught it, thinking about what Celia had said. Her little sister *was* good at drawing, for her age— much better than Tate had been. Now there would be two artists in the Willow family. Tate tried to feel happy about this. She failed.

Abner nudged Tate. "So, what *are* you going to join this year?" he asked again.

There was a hot, prickly feeling behind Tate's eyes. "Nothing," she said. "I'm not good at anything." She tossed up her backpack again. *Thwup!*

She hadn't meant to kick it so hard. The bright green backpack sailed past her hands. It hit a corner of the ledge and hung there, teeter-

ing. Then, as Tate reached for it, the backpack
tipped. *Splash!*

The four Willows ran alongside the river
after the bobbing, twirling backpack.

"Catch it! Catch it!" cried Celia.

"There goes your homework!" Derek shouted.

Abner was the oldest, and he ran the fastest. He caught up with the backpack, but couldn't think how to get it out of the river.

Tate looked ahead. She had an idea. "The big log!" she called, pointing. "You can catch it there!"

The big log was a tree that had fallen long ago. It slanted down into the river, large and partly hollow. On days when the river had been calmer, the Willows had used it for a lookout, a pirate ship, and a desert island.

Abner saw at once what Tate meant. He put on a last burst of speed and climbed out on the big log. He snagged the backpack by its strap as it went past. The tree rocked under his weight. "Whoa," he said, catching hold of the trunk.

Tate arrived at the big log, breathing hard. She could see that the fallen tree was not as steady as it once was. The rising river, pushing hard against the tree, had loosened it from the bank. On the opposite side, water swirled and sucked in a froth of dirty foam.

She looked around. There was a long, thin branch on the ground. "Here!" She picked up the branch and held it out. "Use it for balance, and come on!"

Abner grabbed the branch and skipped off the log in a hurry. He landed on the riverbank with a solid thump. Then he handed the dripping backpack to Tate. "What do you mean, you're not good at anything?" he demanded.

Derek and Celia came running up. They looked at Tate curiously. They wanted to hear the answer, too.

Tate dug in her backpack to see what had gotten wet. Her long brown ponytail swung past her chin.

Abner shook her lightly by the arm. "You're the one who knows how to explain things to grown-ups so we don't get into trouble, remember?"

"And you're *nice*," Celia said. "Abby Downey's big sister is mean, and so is Joey Sisco's. I'm glad you're not like them."

"Thanks," Tate said, sighing. What was she supposed to do—join the Nice Club? The Talking to Grown-ups Club? She pulled out the papers in her backpack. They were damp around the edges.

Derek peeled some of the papers apart and flapped them in the air to dry. "You're good at staying calm when things start *happening*."

Tate tried to dry the backpack with the hem of her shirt. "Calm and nice," she said. "I sound like the world's most boring person."

Derek flopped on the grass beside Tate. "I

mean when *weird* things start happening," he said. "*You* know."

"Like *magic*," Celia said.

"Oh," said Tate.

The Willow children had discovered that there was magic somewhere deep inside Hollowstone Hill. At times, it seeped up and got into things, and then they never knew what would happen. It had gotten into their hamster, an old lawn mower, and even some grasshoppers. And Tate had to admit that they could have gotten into a lot of trouble each time.

But she wasn't talking about magic now. "I meant that I'm not good at anything for *school*," Tate said. "I'm not *smart*."

The others were quiet for a moment. Tate was not the world's best student, it was true. But she worked very hard.

"You like to read," Derek pointed out.

"Hey!" Abner smoothed out the paper he was holding. "Look at this! Why don't you go out for the Book Quiz Team?"

"Yeah!" said Derek. "I heard they went to the state tournament last year!"

Abner read from the paper in his hand. "Tryouts are on Monday. You must have read all the books. There will be a test."

"I won't pass it," said Tate. She reached for

the paper and stuffed it in her backpack. She felt like throwing it in the river, but she didn't want to litter.

Celia said, "Yes, you will! You've been reading books all summer long!"

Tate shook her head. "I've been reading from the list my *old* school gave out. But this school is in a new state. I found out today that their book list is totally different."

There was a little silence. "Wow," said Abner.

Derek jammed his cap low on his head. "Too bad."

Celia gave her big sister a squeeze around the middle. "That's so unfair!"

Tate shrugged. She tried to smile. Then she looked up the hill to their house. "Hey, isn't that Mr. Wopter's truck? What's wrong now?"

CHAPTER 2

A Scary Discovery

Mr. Wopter was a farmer who lived down the road. He was a handyman, too. He drove his dusty blue pickup truck to the Willows' house when things needed fixing.

The truck's tailgate was open. Derek and Celia stood on their tiptoes to see.

"Mr. Wopter sure has a lot of tools," said Derek.

Tate followed Abner up the porch steps.

She wasn't interested in Mr. Wopter's truck. She wanted to tell her mother about the Quiz Team tryouts. She wanted her mother to tell her that it didn't matter, and that things would look better in the morning.

"Oh, good, you're home!" Mrs. Willow picked up a large, flat case. "I'm sorry, kids. I've got to run to town. Someone bought one of my paintings and wants to see more!"

"Wow! Your first sale!" said Abner.

Tate did not share her bad news. Her mother was in a big hurry.

Mrs. Willow gave them both a quick hug, her car keys jingling. "I'll be back," she said. "Be good and don't get in Mr. Wopter's way— he's fixing the pipes." She lowered her voice. "I hope he's done before your father comes home. Your father would try to do it himself."

Abner and Tate looked at one another. They

knew what their mother meant. They had seen their father fix things before. Usually, he made the problem worse.

"Your father tries very hard, of course," said Mrs. Willow quickly.

The children nodded. Their father did try hard. When he decided to fix things, he grunted. He sweated until his shirt was damp. He got out all the tools in his toolbox, and there was a lot of clanking.

"And, of course, he's a very smart man," said Mrs. Willow. "Just look at his work for the university!"

The children nodded again. Their father *was* smart. Everyone knew that. He just wasn't any good at being a handyman. Most times, their mother had to pay someone else to come and fix what their father had fixed.

"Nobody's good at everything," said Tate.

Mr. Wopter's legs stuck out in the middle of the kitchen floor. His head and shoulders were in the cupboard beneath the sink. Now and then, his hand fumbled on the floor for a different tool.

Abner squatted down. "I could hand you the tools," he said.

The front door slammed. Derek and Celia came in from looking at the truck and threw their backpacks on the kitchen table. "What's Mr. Wopter doing?" Celia asked.

"Fixing the pipes," said Abner.

Derek looked at the faucet. "Can we still get a drink?"

Tate didn't want to bother Mr. Wopter. "Maybe we should get a drink from the bathroom faucet," she said.

Mr. Wopter's voice sounded hollow from inside the cupboard. "You can't get a drink from

any faucet until I'm done. I shut off the water
for the whole house."

Abner was curious. "How do you shut off
the water?" he asked.

"Down in the basement, by the meter," said
Mr. Wopter. "Hand me that clamp, will you?"

Small clanking sounds came from under the sink.

"I'm thirsty," said Celia.

Suddenly they were all thirsty. It had been a long, hot walk up the hill.

Tate looked in the refrigerator. "There's milk," she said.

"Is there juice?" Celia asked.

"No. We finished the pitcher this morning," Tate said. She poured out glasses of milk for everyone.

Celia drank her glass in a hurry. Milk clung to her upper lip in a white mustache. "I'm still thirsty," she said.

Everyone wanted another glass. And then the milk carton was empty. Celia turned it up-side down over her mouth to get the last drops, but they splashed on her chin. She wiped off her chin with her hand. Now her hand was sticky, but she couldn't wash it, because there was no water.

Mr. Wopter's hands gripped the edge of the cupboard. He slid himself out and sat up. Then he went to his truck and looked through a box of pipe fittings.

The Willows followed him. "Can we turn on the water yet?" Celia asked.

"Nope." Mr. Wopter dug deeper in the box. There was a sound of clinking metal.

Derek said, "We could get water from the river, with a bucket."

"We'd have to boil the water before we drank it, though," Tate said.

Mr. Wopter straightened up, frowning. "You kids had better stay away from that river. Last year, when it was running this high, it swept away Wilmer Olson's prize pig."

"A whole pig?" said Celia.

"What happened to the pig?" asked Abner. "Did it drown?"

"No, it swam all right. But once it went over the waterfall in town, there wasn't much left but a few pounds of bacon."

The children were silent, imagining this.

Mr. Wopter held up a bit of pipe and squinted at it. "Too bad your folks don't use the old well. If they did, you could go out and pull up a bucket of water right now."

"We have a well?" Abner said. "Where?"

Mr. Wopter scratched under his cap. "See, I don't exactly know. I never used it myself. But this property had to have a well sometime in the past. The people who lived here got water from someplace, didn't they? Back in the day, town water pipes didn't go out this far."

"Why wouldn't they get water from the river?" asked Derek.

"Rivers aren't clean enough. But if you dig a well down past bedrock, you get pure water." Mr. Wopter pulled out a short length of copper pipe from the box in his truck. "Aha! This is what I need."

Celia tugged at his sleeve. "Are you going to be done soon?" The milk had dried on her skin and she felt stickier than ever.

"I'll tell you the truth," said Mr. Wopter. "I'll be done sooner if you all play somewhere else and let me get on with my work."

The Willows watched him go into the house.

"I guess we *were* bothering him," said Celia.

"Maybe *you* were," said Derek.

"*I* wasn't," said Abner. "I was helping. Right, Tate?"

Tate sighed. This was the problem with being calm and nice. People expected her to smooth things over all the time.

"Look," she said. "You were *all* trying to help Mr. Wopter. Let's just drop it and do something else."

"Like what?" Derek demanded.

Tate wondered why she had to think of everything. She felt just as grumpy as the others. And she was still thirsty.

Still thirsty? Suddenly Tate had an idea. "Let's find the well!"

There was a moment of silence as the glory of this plan sank in.

"I'll get a bucket!" Abner took off for the shed.

"I'll get a rope!" Derek shouted, running after him.

"Wait for me!" cried Celia. "I want to help!"

❧❧❧

But they couldn't find it. They looked in the front yard and they looked in the back. They looked behind the garden shed, the toolshed, and the garage, and past the ring of trees at the crown of the hill. They dragged the bucket and rope everywhere they went. But they didn't see anything that seemed to be an old well.

Tate stepped up onto a large, flat rock on the crest of the hill. "There's one place we haven't looked," she said.

The others climbed up beside her and looked down at the wild side of Hollowstone Hill.

This side was steep. It was rocky. It was covered with sticker bushes and thistles, and sharp branches that had blown off trees. It had a heap of old, rusted metal that their mother had told them was dangerous. And there was a rock pile that their father had said might be a den for snakes.

This worried Celia. "I'm not going anywhere that has snakes," she said.

Tate saw a big stick on the ground. She

swung it across the weeds. "This will keep the snakes away."

Derek stuck his hands in his pockets. "I went down there once," he said. "It took me a whole hour to pick the stickers off my jeans."

Abner said, "We don't really need to find the well. I bet Mr. Wopter's done fixing the pipes." He picked up the rope and looped it over his arm.

But Tate didn't want to give up just to make everyone happy. She wanted to run, and yell, and bash things with a stick. For once, she didn't care about being nice or calm.

So she jumped off the big rock, ran down the steep hill, and leaped onto a bramble-covered mound.

"I'm the queen of the mountain!" she cried, stomping her foot. "I'm the queen of Hollow-stone H—"

Crrraaaaack.

For one brief moment, Tate's startled face looked up at her brothers and sister. And then there was an even louder crack, like a door breaking into pieces, and Tate went *down*. Her hair flew up, and the rest of her went down in a violent cracking of rotten wood. There was a faint sound, like the distant echo of a scream, and then silence.

Tate had found the well.

CHAPTER 3

It Might Be Magic

Abner stood frozen on the big, flat rock. He could not seem to think, or move, or make a sound. Beside him, Derek and Celia were stiff, their mouths open.

Then Abner took charge. "Celia. Run to the house and get Mr. Wopter. *Run.*"

Celia ran.

"Come on," Abner said to Derek. "We've got to throw her the rope. *Hurry.*"

The boys smashed through sticker bushes and thistles, but they didn't notice their scratches. They reached the well, breathing hard, and leaned over the rim. The well was narrow and deep in shadow.

"Tate! TATE!" they shouted, their voices echoing.

There was no answer.

Derek looked at Abner, stricken.

"She's there. She's just catching her breath." Abner pulled Derek back. "Don't lean too far. And don't push any more of that rotted wood in. It might fall on her head."

"Aren't you going to throw down the rope?"

"I'll tie it to something first." Abner knotted the rope around a thorn tree. He brushed away the broken wood from the well. Then he lowered the loose end of the rope.

The boys leaned over the edge, hardly

breathing. The inside of the well smelled cold
and damp, like moss on wet stone, and it went
down farther than they could see.

"Did you hear a splash?" Derek asked.

Abner strained his ears. "Maybe."

"*TATE!*" they yelled together.

Celia came up, panting.

Abner whipped around. Where was Mr. Wopter?

Celia held out a note. "I couldn't read it. Mr. Wopter's writing is too slanty." She squeezed her stuffed rabbit to her heart. She had seen Mr. Bunny as she ran through the front hall and grabbed him. She needed something to hug when she was scared.

Abner snatched the paper and read it with a sinking heart. Mr. Wopter's note said he was going to town to get a pipe fitting.

"What does it say?" demanded Derek.

"It says he'll be back soon," said Abner. He looked at his brother and sister hopelessly. It would not be soon enough.

❧❧❧

Dark. Cold. Wet. Water was all around Tate, in her nose and in her eyes. She tried to swim but she didn't know which way was up. Her foot knocked into something hard. Her elbow scraped against something rough. She couldn't think of anything except that she had to breathe. Air, she needed air! But she opened her mouth, and there was only water.

Almost by accident, she opened her eyes. There, high above, was a faint circle of light. She kicked her legs, and her head broke the surface of the water. She gasped once, twice, but she forgot to keep kicking. She went down.

She kicked hard and came up choking. She knew she shouldn't panic, but she didn't know what else to do. She couldn't tread water. She had tried to learn in her last swimming class, and she had failed the test.

She flung her hands out and they touched something slimy. Was it the wall? Was it a dead fish? Was it something worse? She shuddered, and her head went under while she was still trying to breathe. Water was in her nose, in her mouth, choking her. The water in the well swirled around her and she started to sink for the third time.

And then, all at once, something was different.

She stopped being afraid. She started to think. All at once, she could remember everything her swimming instructor had said, and it made perfect sense.

Cup the hands. Move the arms wide and back. Kick in a big crossing motion. And do everything in the right order, making arms and legs work together.

She hadn't been able to keep it all straight in swimming class. But now treading water was easy!

Tate's head popped above water, and she

looked up. She could see a circle of blue, with two heads looking down. The faces were in shadow, but she knew they were her brothers.

The bigger figure motioned with his arm. "GRAB THE ROPE!" Abner shouted. *"Rope! Rope! Rope!"* The word echoed in the well, and Tate could see the dangling end of a rope, five feet above her.

Tate called up between breaths, "IT'S . . . TOO . . . SHORT!"

The two heads above looked at one another in despair.

Tate didn't know why they were upset. The answer was simple. "GET . . . ANOTHER . . . ROPE . . . AND . . . TIE . . . IT . . . ON!"

The heads disappeared. Tate kept on treading water. She bumped into large pieces of the well cover that had fallen with her. They were made of wood, so they floated.

Her mind was still sharp and clear. She had a good idea.

Tate stacked the pieces on top of each other and wrapped her arms around them. Then she rested her chin on top and let herself float. The pieces of wood held her up, and she could rest.

She heard her little sister's voice, yelling something. Tate couldn't understand what it was because of the echo. She looked up in time to see something coming at her, growing larger . . . something with *ears*. . . .

Mr. Bunny bounced off her head with a soft thump, then a splash. He looked at her with his button eyes and slowly began to sink.

Tate laughed. Celia thought Mr. Bunny would help her be brave while she waited for rescue. But Tate would have to rescue Mr. Bunny. He was soaking up water like a sponge.

She tucked the waterlogged rabbit inside

her shirt and looked up calmly at the circle of blue sky. And then she noticed that the well was made of big gray bricks. Some of the bricks stuck out a little. Was there a way she could climb up?

Her stick had fallen into the well with her and was floating nearby. Tate saw at once how she could use it.

It was strange, how quickly the ideas were coming to her! There must be some bricks sticking out below, too. Tate felt around until she found edges where she could put her feet. She took the stick and wedged the tip against a brick that stuck out on the opposite side of the well. The stick helped her balance. It was as if she were a three-legged stool, with the stick being one of the legs. She straightened her knees and slowly stood up. Now she was half-way out of the water!

She could probably climb all the way out if she had to. But the stick might break. And anyway, here came the rope, tumbling onto her head. Far above, her brothers and sister looked down at her.

Tate knotted the rope around her body. Then she gave it a tug. "PULL—A—LITTLE—AT—A—TIME!" she yelled. "ONLY—PULL—WHEN—I—SAY!"

The biggest head nodded violently. Good—that meant Abner understood. Step by step, Tate found a foothold and wedged her stick. She yelled, "PULL!" The rope tightened. She stepped up a foot, and then another.

It wasn't long before she was at the top. With one final effort, Tate climbed over the lip of the well and rolled onto solid ground.

The Willows leaned against each other, their backs to the well. No one said anything for a minute. They were all breathing too hard. But Celia had climbed onto Tate's lap and was holding on as if she would never let her sister go.

"Well, *that* was interesting," said Abner at last.

"No kidding," Derek said.

Celia hugged her sister tight. "I was scared, Tate."

"I was, too," Tate admitted. "But then all of a sudden, I wasn't."

She tumbled Celia off her lap and stood up. Tate's mind was going so fast that she couldn't stay still. There wasn't enough for it to do.

"I want to go do my homework," she said, and skipped up the hill.

"What?" Abner jumped up. "You almost *drowned*, and now you want to *do your homework*?"

"Why not?" Tate leaped over the big, flat rock.

Abner, Derek, and Celia trudged after her, dragging the ropes and bucket. "I don't get it," said Abner. "You'd think she'd be tired, after all that swimming and climbing."

"Look!" said Derek.

The Willows stared. Tate was doing cartwheels. At first, they were wobbly, as usual. But each one got better. Soon she was doing them as if she had practiced every day for a year!

Next, she tried a flip.

"She can't do that," said Abner slowly.

"She just did," Celia pointed out.

"I know," Abner said. "But what I mean is, she's never been that good before. Don't you remember how Mom signed her up for gymnastics last year, and her cartwheels were all crooked? And she could barely do a flip without falling over."

"Wow, she did it again!" Derek shouted. "It's like she's learning in fast motion!"

They watched in silence as Tate did three more flips in a row. She stopped at the clothesline by the garden, pulled Celia's stuffed rabbit from her shirt, and hung him up to dry. Then she leaped over the porch railing, swung around the post like a monkey, and dashed through the front door. Faintly, in the distance, they heard it slam.

The Willows looked at one another.

"That wasn't normal for Tate," said Abner.

"That was just plain *weird*," Derek said.

Celia gazed at Mr. Bunny, dangling on the line with clothespins in his ears. "It might be magic," she said.

CHAPTER 4

Safety Last

They followed Tate's damp footprints down the hall and up the stairs to the third floor.

This was the Loft, and it was all theirs. The boys shared a bedroom at one end of the floor, and the girls were at the other end. In between was a long room with a slanted ceiling, five windows, and plenty of space to do whatever they wanted.

Oddly, it seemed that what Tate wanted to

do was homework. She had not even changed into dry clothes. She was sprawled on the wooden floor. Her math book was open and she was solving problems.

"Why isn't she waiting until Sunday night?" whispered Derek. "I always do."

Abner squinted at Tate's paper. She was doing long division. The problems did not look simple.

"Done!" Tate slammed the book and reached for another. "Now I just have to read one chapter in history and answer some questions."

"She's turning those pages awfully fast," said Derek.

Abner was worried about Tate. Falling down the well had changed her. She *couldn't* be reading her history book that fast—could she?

Tate slammed her history book shut. She put her answer sheets in her backpack, ready for school on Monday. Then she looked around for something else to do.

Derek's scouting handbook was on the floor, open to the page on knots. She scanned the pictures. "Hmm," she said. "Bowline, slip-knot, reef knot . . ." She studied the bowline knot. It was strong enough to tow a heavy boat, yet could be untied easily.

Abner squatted down. "Tate," he said carefully, "how do you feel?"

"Amazing!" She flung out her arms. Drops of water sprayed from her wet sleeves. "I feel like I could do all the homework in the world, and it would be fun!"

"Want to do mine?" Derek asked.

"No, she doesn't," said Abner. "Listen, Tate. What really happened to you, down in that well? Because you're acting a little—"

"Funny?" said Celia.

"Mental?" said Derek.

"Unusual," Abner finished. "We think there was magic in the well. You were swimming in it."

Tate bounced on her toes. "It feels like my brain has speeded up. It's like I can think faster and remember more and learn without hardly trying."

Derek grinned. "You learned how to do a flip awfully fast."

"You did your homework in about five minutes, too," Abner said.

"Cool," said Tate. "I guess I'll help everybody else do theirs, then. Homework is fun!"

Everyone stared at her.

Derek backed away a step. "I think I'll just practice tying knots." He picked up a piece of twine and sat on the couch. He looked nervously at Tate out of the corner of his eye.

Celia said, "I'm going to color. That's sort of like homework, don't you think?" She ran to the craft table and took out a box of crayons.

Abner cleared his throat. This was a Tate he didn't understand. "Don't you want to change clothes? You're dripping." He pointed at the floor, where a small puddle was forming.

Tate looked at it in surprise. "Wow, more water! That's wild!" She stamped her foot happily, making a little splash.

"Tate," said Abner firmly, giving his sister a nudge toward her bedroom. "Go. Change into dry clothes. And then—I don't know, read a book or something."

Tate stiffened. Her eyes lit up. "I know! I could read TEN books!"

She dug in her backpack for the crumpled book list Mr. Davy had handed out. "Do we have any of these on our bookshelves? Hurry and look, everybody! And let's bike to the library for the rest. I'm going to read them *all* before Monday!"

They found four of the books in the house. Then they rode their bikes down the hill and over the stone arch bridge. Derek whizzed ahead on the country road. Abner pedaled standing up. Celia sat behind him and held on tight.

"Hey!" she shouted. "Look at Tate!"

Tate had gotten off her bike at the bridge. She was taking off her shoes and socks.

Abner and Derek rode back in a hurry. "Are you nuts?" Abner demanded. "You can't go wading."

"Look how high the river is!" Derek said.

"Mr. Wopter told us it was dangerous," Celia added.

"It doesn't look dangerous," said Tate. "It looks fun!"

"It probably looked fun to Wilmer Olson's prize pig, too," Derek said. "Until it went over the falls."

"Tate!" Abner shook her shoulders. "Library! Book Quiz Team! Remember?"

"Oh, right," said Tate. She leaned toward the river a little.

Celia reached up to put her hands over

Tate's eyes. "Just don't look at the water."

This seemed to work. Tate didn't know where the river was when her eyes were covered.

Abner had an idea. He whispered in Celia's ear, "Go piggyback. Play Warmer, Colder to get her across the bridge." He boosted Celia onto Tate's back.

"I love this game!" said Tate. She took a step toward the river.

"Colder!" cried Celia.

Tate took a step toward the bridge, then another.

"Warmer!" Celia said. "Almost hot! Boiling!"

Abner and Derek wheeled Tate's bike across the bridge. Then they made Tate get on her bike and go ahead so they could watch her. The dust from the road spat up behind her wheels and made a hazy cloud.

"Wow, look at her go!" Derek said.

"Doesn't she *ever* get tired?" said Celia.

"WAIT!" Abner shouted.

They caught up to Tate at the edge of town. She was riding her bike back and forth through a sprinkler on someone's lawn.

The house's front door opened. A bald man

put his head out. "Hey, you! Get off my grass!"

Abner felt his face flushing red. "Come *on*, Tate!"

Tate swooped off the lawn. "Did you know that if you ride through a sprinkler with the sun at your back, you can see a rainbow? Isn't water amazing?"

"Yeah, amazing," said Abner glumly.

On the next block, Tate splashed her hands in someone's birdbath. And on the block after that, she put on the brakes when she saw a kiddie pool in a yard.

"NO!" Abner tried to head her off.

"You don't want to swim with *toddlers*," Derek said. "No telling what they'll do in the water."

Tate looked suddenly wary. "Oh, right."

Abner saw a row of willow trees ahead. He suddenly remembered that they lined the river where it went through town.

"This way!" He pointed firmly to the left.

They turned onto Main Street. When they rode past the hardware store, Abner was glad to see a dusty blue truck full of tools. He felt better knowing Mr. Wopter was nearby, just in case.

They were as thirsty as a desert. The small

entry to the library had a drinking fountain, and everyone took a good, long drink. Tate turned the water on full force. The water squirted all over the floor.

Abner looked helplessly at Derek. He didn't think he could yell at Tate in a *library*.

Oddly, it was Celia who knew what to do. She held out her hand to Tate. "Come on," she said. "Don't you want to pick out your books? Don't you want to read them all and make the Quiz Team?"

"Yes," said Tate, "but look at the way the water drops splash! Every one is different!"

"Books are even more different," said Celia, and she tugged Tate into the library.

Abner watched the big double doors close behind his sisters. Then he turned to Derek. "Get some paper towels and mop this up, will you?"

"What are you going to do?" asked Derek.

"I'm going to the hardware store. Maybe Mr. Wopter will give us a ride home in his truck. That will keep Tate out of water trouble."

"Brilliant," said Derek with feeling.

Mr. Wopter was not at the hardware store. He had gone to the pie shop next door for something to eat.

"Sure, I'll take you home," he said. "Just let me finish my coffee, and I'll swing by and load your bikes in the truck."

When Abner got back to the library, Derek and Celia were stacking books in the bike baskets.

"Where's Tate?" Abner asked.

Celia looked around. "She was here a minute ago."

"TATE!" yelled Abner, cupping his hands around his mouth.

No one answered.

Derek cocked his head. "Do you hear water?"

Celia gasped.

"Oh, *no*," said Abner. He suddenly remembered that the river ran some distance behind the library, through a park with trails—and over a cliff.

They left their bikes. They left the books. They raced down a trail, along a bend in the river, past a bench and a drinking fountain and a picnic table—and made it to the falls just in time to see Tate climbing over the guardrail.

Abner grabbed Tate's right arm. Derek grabbed her left. Celia got a good grip on Tate's ankles and hung on tight.

"Oh, come *on*," Tate said. "I was just going to look."

"You can see plenty from right here," said

Abner. "Like, did you notice the thirty-foot drop? Onto rocks?"

"I wasn't going to fall," Tate protested.

"You're not going to fall *now*," Abner said grimly. "Pull, everybody!"

Tate stumbled backward. "You get a better view up close," she protested.

No one bothered to answer. They marched

her back to the bikes and didn't let go until she was on the truck, with a book in her hand. And when Mr. Wopter dropped them off at the stone arch bridge, they borrowed his handkerchief for a blindfold.

☯☯☯

Tate was upstairs in the Loft, already on her third book. Abner, Derek, and Celia sat on the stairs, talking things over.

"That was weird," Derek said. "I mean, a *kiddie pool*? Get serious!"

"I'm worried about the river," said Abner. "If she gets too close—"

"Whoosh! Over the falls!" said Derek. "Just like the pig."

Celia's lower lip trembled. "I don't want Tate to land on the rocks."

Abner gave her a hug. "She won't," he said. "Reading books will keep her busy for a long time. We just have to stand guard at the door."

"Let's keep her away from all kinds of water," Derek said. "So she doesn't go wild."

"Or get reminded of the river," said Celia.

Abner nodded. He had not forgotten that thirty-foot drop over the falls, or the wickedly sharp rocks at the bottom.

"The magic will wear off, won't it?" asked Celia. "After a while?"

Abner fervently hoped so. "It always has before," he said.

Mrs. Willow came home. She wanted to know why the carpet was damp.

Abner, Derek, and Celia explained about the well. Their mother gave a little shriek. "Is Tate all right? Where is she?"

"The Loft," said Abner, "but—"

Mrs. Willow didn't stay to hear the rest. She

ran up the stairs, and her children ran after her.

Tate let her mother check her for bruises, hug her, and smooth her hair. Then she picked up her book again.

Mrs. Willow walked to the door. She looked back. "She seems to be all right," she said. "But she's turning the pages too fast to be really reading. I suppose she's just trying not to think about that dreadful fall."

Celia said, "It's more like she's thinking *faster*— Ow!" She stopped as Derek nudged her in the ribs with his elbow.

Soon it was time for supper. "Can Tate have her supper on a tray?" Abner asked his parents. "She wants to keep reading."

Mrs. Willow was worried. But Mr. Willow said they should let her alone. "She'll get over it sooner if we let her handle it in her own way. And listen, you kids. I don't want you going anywhere near that well until we get a cover on it."

Mrs. Willow looked in the refrigerator. "We're out of milk."

The children glanced at one another guiltily.

"The water was shut off for a long time," said Abner.

"We were really thirsty," Celia said.

"Oh, well," said their mother. "We'll drink water with supper. I'll make juice in the morning, and we can have bacon and eggs instead of cereal."

"Water?" said Derek. He glanced at Abner and Celia.

"Can Tate have a soda?" Abner asked quickly. "For a special treat, because she fell?"

Mother smiled. "Oh, just this once."

It was long past their bedtime when Tate closed the sixth book on her list. Derek and Celia were asleep. Even Mr. and Mrs. Willow had gone to bed, but Abner was staying awake to watch Tate.

He yawned widely. His eyelids drooped. "Are you going to bed?" he mumbled.

Tate nodded. "I'm just going to get a drink first."

No one liked to drink from the bathroom faucet, because it tasted of toothpaste. Abner watched in a sleepy daze as Tate started down the stairs. His eyes drifted shut.

Then, all at once, they snapped open. Was she going to get a drink of *water*?

Th-thump!

The sound came from below. Abner ran down the steps. Now there was a spurting, spraying sound. He rounded the corner to see Tate squatting on the kitchen counter with the spray hose

in her hand. She was spraying water up into her mouth. She was getting everything wet.

"Tate, STOP!" he hissed.

Tate, startled, jerked back. One foot slipped into the sink. She lost her balance and fell right onto the faucet.

It broke off. Water sprayed everywhere. And no matter how Tate twisted the faucet handles, the water just kept shooting out.

CHAPTER 5

Water in the Night

Abner's whisper was furious. "Now look what you've done! What were you doing on the counter?"

"I was checking the water flow!" Tate's whisper was every bit as mad. "I wouldn't have fallen if you hadn't scared me!"

Water sprayed everywhere. Abner slipped on the wet floor and grabbed the counter's edge. "Think of something! You're the one who's so smart!"

"My brain isn't smarter. It's just faster," Tate snapped. She looked around, thinking hard. The first thing was to stop the water.

She grabbed a dish towel and pressed it on the hole where the faucet had been. The towel was soaked, but at least the water wasn't spraying all over.

Then Tate had another idea. "In the basement, by the meter," she said.

"What?"

"That's what Mr. Wopter said when you asked him how to shut off the water. Remember?" She pressed the towel harder against the hole. The water pushed around her fingers and squirted into her face.

"Right!" Abner ran downstairs. Where was the meter? Was it that round thing with dials? There was a handle next to it. He turned the handle and hoped for the best.

Up in the kitchen, the stream of water became a trickle and stopped. Tate felt a little sad. Something in her loved to see the water spraying free. But another part of her brain knew she was in big trouble.

"Well done," said Tate when Abner came back to the kitchen. She wrung out the sopping towel. "Now we have to mop up the water. Look—isn't it kind of cool, the way it flows over the floor?"

Abner grunted. Then he grabbed a mop from the closet. "*I'll* clean up. You go to bed. And stay away from water until the magic wears off, will you?"

Tate sighed as she climbed the steps. She was pretty sure the magic was starting to wear off already. It had taken her longer to read that last book. Maybe she had better read the seventh one before the magic was completely gone.

Tate lay in bed with her reading light on. She heard Abner come up the stairs. Then she heard his bedsprings creak.

She tried to read. But she couldn't keep her mind on her book.

The magic had felt so wonderful at first! She had actually enjoyed doing her homework—it was fun to understand things so quickly. She had felt as if she could learn anything at all! Not just out of books, but things like cartwheels and flips and treading water, too. But she had done some stupid things.

At the waterfall, she had scared her brothers and sister. She had made a watery mess at the library. And now she had broken the kitchen faucet.

Her parents would have to pay Mr. Wopter to fix it. They would have to pay someone to cover the old well, too.

Everything she'd done had caused trouble. Everything she'd done would cost money to fix.

And now her family wouldn't have anything to drink in the morning. They were out of milk. And they wouldn't have water to make coffee or juice until the faucet was fixed.

Her parents would be grouchy enough when they saw the broken faucet. They would be even grouchier without their coffee. And everyone would be thirsty.

Suddenly Tate sat up in bed. She knew where there was water.

She shivered. Did she dare? Did she dare go out at night, in the dark, to the wild side of Hollowstone Hill?

Tate put on a robe over her pajamas. She put on her shoes and socks. Then she found the flashlight they kept in the Loft in case the power went out.

She crept past the room where the boys were sleeping. She tiptoed down the stairs, skipping the step that squeaked. She opened the front door.

Abner had left the bucket and rope on the porch. She slung the rope over one shoulder in a coil. She didn't feel like doing any flips. Her mind was busy enough, watching for rocks, gopher holes, and wild animals that might be out at night.

It was chilly. The grass was damp. Overhead was a thin, sharp moon. The flashlight beam didn't go very far. Tate stood shivering on the big, flat rock at the crest of the hill and looked down. The wild side of the hill was even scarier at night.

Her mind might have been going five times faster, but that didn't mean she was five times braver. Tate did not want to go down

into the steep, prickly dark.

The first step was the hardest. After that, she just kept going. Her robe was full of stickers by the time she found the well.

She leaned her flashlight against a thorn tree. She tied the bucket on the rope, using the bowline knot she had just studied. Then she remembered something she had learned in school. If she threw the rope over a tree branch, it would act as a simple pulley. She could pull the loose end of the rope to lift the bucket. It would be easier.

Tate lowered the bucket until she heard it hit the water. When she felt the bucket grow heavy, she pulled on the rope.

It was hard work to pull a bucket of water all the way up the well. Even though she was using a tree branch as a pulley, it took a long time.

It was even harder to lug a bucket of water back to the house. Some of the water sloshed out. She had to stop and rest when her hands got sore.

But she had done it! She had gotten water for her family!

Tate opened the refrigerator. Her mother had put in a can of frozen juice to thaw for the morning. The directions on the label said to mix with three cans of water. That was easy. Tate got out a pitcher and made the juice.

Then she looked at the coffeemaker. It had directions, too. She scooped out the coffee. She measured the water and poured it in. All she had to do in the morning was push the button to ON.

Tate climbed the stairs to the Loft, yawning. She was so tired. Her mind seemed slower, too. The magic was almost gone.

Tate turned out her light and shut her eyes. She had read six books out of the ten on Mr. Davy's list. That left four still to read before Monday.

Without magic, she didn't have a chance.

☙☙☙

Sunshine seeped in between the window and the shade. Tate opened her eyes. Celia was still sleeping.

Tate threw on jeans and a shirt and ran downstairs. Were her parents up yet? She had to push the button on the coffeemaker. If her parents were greeted by the smell of fresh coffee, maybe they wouldn't be so mad about the broken faucet.

Tate ran to get the newspaper. By the time her parents came downstairs, the coffee was hot.

Tate poured them each a cup. "Hi, Mom! Hi, Dad!"

Mr. and Mrs. Willow looked surprised. Mr. Willow smiled, took his coffee, and picked up the paper.

"I'll drink mine in a minute, Tate," said Mrs.

Willow. "I promised to make everyone bacon and eggs."

Derek and Abner were watching cartoons in the next room. Tate stood in the doorway, biting her fingernails. If her parents didn't notice the broken faucet soon, she would have to tell them.

Her mother opened the refrigerator. She saw the pitcher of juice. "Did you make juice, too, Tate? Thank you!"

Tate took a deep breath.

But Mother had already started to talk to Father. She said that someone wanted to buy more of her paintings. She kept talking while she got out the frying pan and put in the bacon.

The bacon began to sizzle. Mrs. Willow cracked eggs into the pan. She was still talking, and Tate hadn't had a chance to tell her anything.

"Boys! Breakfast!" Mother called. She went to the sink to wash her hands. Then she gasped. "What happened to the faucet?"

It took a long time to explain.

"Let me get this straight," said Mr. Willow. "You were up on the counter? Can you tell me why you thought that was a good idea?"

Tate shook her head miserably. She stood up to pour the juice. Maybe if she was helpful enough, her parents wouldn't be so mad.

Celia came down the stairs in her pajamas. "Can I have some juice, too?"

Mother looked at the pitcher in Tate's hand. "Wait a minute."

Tate didn't like the tone of her mother's voice.

"If the faucet broke last night," Mother said, "where did you get the water to make juice? And coffee?"

Tate explained about the well. Before she even finished, her mother cried, "Don't drink that juice!" She dumped the whole pitcher down the drain.

Tate stared at her mother. Why had she done that?

"We don't know how safe that water is," said Mrs. Willow. "You might have gotten sick from it."

"But I used it to make coffee, too," Tate whispered.

Her father looked at his coffee cup. "Oh, well." He drank the last swallow. "Go ahead and drink yours, Molly—I'm sure the coffee is hot enough to kill any germs."

Mrs. Willow looked at her cup doubtfully. "I suppose so."

"But what are *we* going to drink?" asked Derek. "This bacon is salty, and I'm thirsty."

Mr. Willow said, "You can have coffee, too." He grinned at his wife. "Don't worry, Molly. Coffee isn't going to hurt them this once."

Celia took a sip of coffee. She made a face.

"Cool!" said Derek. Coffee was a grown-up drink.

Abner didn't like coffee, but it was partly his fault that the faucet had broken. He supposed he deserved to drink something bitter with breakfast.

Tate didn't drink her coffee. She felt too terrible.

"It's excellent coffee, too," said their father. He flung out his arms and did a little tap dance. "It makes me want to get up and *do* something!"

"Good," said their mother. "Because the garden needs weeding, and the gutter needs fixing, and the garage needs cleaning—"

Mr. Willow laughed. "I'll get to all of that," he promised. "But first I want to go to the university. I just had the most wonderful idea, and I want to set up an experiment!"

Mrs. Willow poured herself a cup of coffee. "Oh, my, this *is* good coffee," she said. She drank it all and set her cup down. "I think I'm going to paint today," she said. "Goodness, I can hardly wait to get started! I can't even sit still!"

Mrs. Willow did a little jig out the door and slammed it with her foot.

Tate set down her coffee cup. Then she went to the window. Out on the lawn, her mother was doing a cartwheel.

Tate turned slowly to face the others.

"You're not going to believe this," said Derek, "but I feel like doing homework!"

CHAPTER 6

Danger!

Abner jumped up. "Tate, the magic came be-cause you *drank* the water! Not because you swam in it!"

Tate remembered how she had almost drowned in the well. "I guess I did swallow some water when my head was under," she said.

Abner grinned. "I've got a science project to do that's supposed to take a month. I bet I could get it done before lunch!"

"I'm going to practice my knots," said Derek. "I can finally learn that old bowline knot. And the timber hitch, and the square lashing . . ."

Celia bounced on her toes. "I want to draw a fish! And an octopus! And a shark!"

Tate knew what drinkable magic could do. "Just make sure you don't do anything wild and crazy around water," she warned. "It's better to stay away from it. Now leave me alone, everybody. I'm going to drink my coffee. And then I'm going to read the last four books on my list!"

☙☜☙

Tate flopped back on the living room couch and dropped the eighth book on the floor. It had been so good! Now she only had two stories to go. But maybe she had better check on the others first.

Her brothers and sister weren't in the Loft.

Tate looked out one of the third-story windows. She could see a curve of the river, still muddy and brown from the rains. Would they have gone to the river? No, of course not. Not after yesterday, when they had tried so hard to keep Tate out of danger.

There was a glint of metal down by the stone arch bridge. Their bikes were still where Mr. Wopter had dropped them off yesterday. No one had wanted to bring a bike up the long hill after the tiring trip to the library.

Tate called through the house, but no one answered. She went outside and opened the door to the hut her mother used as a studio.

Mrs. Willow was painting wildly. She had two brushes in each hand and one in her mouth.

"Mom?" said Tate, alarmed.

Her mother turned and smiled, still holding the brush between her teeth.

"Have you seen Abner and Derek and Celia?"

"Mmmph gningy!" Mother shook her head. Drops of paint spattered on her shirt.

"Okay," said Tate, backing up. As she closed the door, she saw her mother kick off a sandal and put a paintbrush between her toes.

Where could the others have gone? Maybe they were in the basement and hadn't heard her calling.

Tate was suddenly inspired to do a good deed. She would bring all the bikes up to the garage! That would help make up for what she had done yesterday.

She whistled as she skipped down the driveway. Today was different from the day before. She was reading just as fast. But she'd been good at staying away from water. Maybe she had just needed a day to get used to drinkable magic, that was all.

Tate reached the river. She dragged her bike up on the bank, away from the water that lapped at its tires. Wait—what was Derek's scouting book doing on the ground? And here was the long rope they had used to pull her out of the well yesterday. Derek must have been using it to practice his knots.

She put the book into her bike basket. Then she coiled the rope on top. Derek should know better than to leave a book on the damp grass.

But where *was* Derek? And where were the others?

A flutter of motion downstream caught her attention. Tate shaded her eyes with her hand. There! They were all playing on the big log.

She frowned. The fallen log wasn't safe, not anymore. Abner should know that. He'd been on it yesterday, and it had been unsteady. And the river had been pushing and pushing at it, all night long. . . .

But Abner would be just as reckless around water today as she had been yesterday. Why hadn't she kept better watch over them all? She should have known that they would go to the river!

Tate dropped her bike and started running. She waved her arms. "GET OFF!" she called.

Abner, Derek, and Celia waved back wildly.

"CLIMB ON!" shouted Abner.

"THIS IS SO FUN!" yelled Derek.

"THE WATER IS SWIRLY!" cried Celia.

For a moment, Tate was tempted to join them. The water *was* swirly! It *did* look fun! She longed to give in to the wild water magic that was still inside her.

But if she did, then who would keep her brothers and sister safe?

"LOOK!" shouted Derek. "THE LOG CAN BOUNCE!"

Tate gasped. "DON'T! IT'S DANGER-OUS!"

But the others were already rocking their bodies up and down. The big log, buoyed up by the river, bobbed and swayed. With a sud-

den *crack*, its roots gave way. The log slid out from the sodden riverbank, rolling sideways. Abner, Derek, and Celia scrabbled at the bark with their hands for a long moment. Then they slipped into the river. Their heads went under.

Tate stood perfectly still for one frozen second. It felt like forever. Then, in the next moment, she was thinking faster than she ever had before. She was on her bike and riding across the bridge like the wind, before she was aware of having thought at all.

There was no time to go for her mother. By the time she ran up the hill, explained everything, and ran back down, her sister and brothers would be far downstream. If only her father hadn't taken the car! A car was much faster than a bike.

But a bike could go faster than the river. Tate could tell by the floating twigs she passed. The river was running four miles an hour—maybe five. She could bike ten miles in an hour, she was pretty sure. And with water magic inside her, she could go even faster.

Tate gasped with relief when she saw three

heads surface. She put on even more speed, racing beyond them. When she had gotten well in the lead, she looked for a branch.

She found something better—an old plank, fallen from a fence. She dragged it to the water's edge and narrowed her eyes, thinking. She threw a smaller branch into the river and watched how the current took it. Then she waited for the right moment.

"Grab on!" she shouted, and pushed the plank far into the stream.

Abner was holding Celia up. Derek had a grip on Abner's shirt. They all were moving their arms and legs to stay afloat. They didn't look afraid. They looked like they were having fun.

Tate clenched her hands together. Water magic was like that. But the danger was still real. She had learned that yesterday.

Abner grabbed the plank. Then the others stretched their arms across it. "Thanks!" they yelled.

Tate got back on her bike and tore ahead. The rope was still in her basket. When she was far enough ahead again, she stopped and took out the rope. She looped one end around her body and got ready.

Her toss was perfect. The rope landed right on the plank, and Abner grabbed it with one hand.

But the current was too strong. He couldn't hold the weight of three people against the whole flow of the river. Tate couldn't, either. Their weight dragged her along, and she fell to the ground. The rope slipped out of Abner's hand.

Tate never knew how she got back on her bike. Suddenly she was riding, with one end of the rope still around her body, and the rest bouncing behind in the dust of the road. If only someone would drive by and help! But the country road was deserted.

Tate pulled the rope into her basket and pedaled faster than she ever had before. She had to ride far, far ahead. She had to give herself enough time to figure out some way to save them. And she had to do it before they came to the waterfall.

Tate's breath was coming in wheezing gasps when she finally made it to the little park above the waterfall. It was right in town—surely there would be somebody here! But there was no one at the picnic table, no one drinking from the fountain, and no one coming along the trail.

Think! Think! If her mind was going so much faster, why couldn't it come up with a way to save her brothers and sister?

And then, all at once, it did.

Tate turned over the picnic table with a strength she didn't know she had. She tied one end of her rope to its legs, and the other end to the drinking fountain. She pulled the table down the slope to the river, just above the bend. Then she watched, her heart beating fast

and hard, for three heads to round a bend farther upriver.

Sweat rolled into her eyes. She blinked. She
almost pushed the table into the current when
she saw a moving shadow of a bird, but she
stopped in time.

There they were! Three bobbing heads, three pairs of arms still gripping the plank. With a strong shove, she launched the upside-down table into the river like a boat, and leaped in. The current carried the table out past the lower bend, into the middle of the river. Was she out far enough? Or would the current carry the others past her?

"KICK HARD!" Tate shouted, against the roar of the falls.

There was a flurry of white foam behind Abner, Derek, and Celia as their feet kicked up a spray of water. *Thud!* They crashed into the table. Tate hauled Celia in by her hair, and Derek and Abner scrambled onto the table, gasping. It sank beneath their weight, but only by a couple of inches. It still held them up.

The wooden plank floated down the river,

tilted for a moment at the cliff's edge, and disappeared over the falls.

The current swung the table downstream.
The rope held it tight and snubbed it into the
bank. The Willows stumbled onto the shore,
holding the rope. Everyone was safe.

CHAPTER 7

Soggy Magic

Perhaps the magic had lost some of its strength, sitting in the coffeemaker all night. Whatever the reason, it wore off faster this time.

For the rest of the weekend, Tate read the ninth book. She didn't play, or even watch when Mr. Wopter covered the well. At supper on Saturday, she heard that her father's experiment (with water) was going well. And her mother had finished three paintings (they were watercolors). But then Tate picked up her book again. She read late into the night, and all of Sunday except for at church. Although the magic was gone, she still felt she had to try. She had been through too much to give up now.

By bedtime on Sunday, she only had one chapter to go. She curled up on the couch in the Loft and kept reading, past ten o'clock. The lamp cast a golden glow on the book in her lap as she turned the final page and read "The End."

Tate gave a deep sigh. *A Wrinkle in Time* had been the best of all. Even if she didn't make the Quiz Team, it would have been worth it, just to read that story.

She looked at the clock on the wall.

She hadn't wanted to give up. She had tried to pretend she could read book number ten in time for the test on Monday. But now she had to admit that she couldn't.

Bedsprings creaked in the boys' room. Abner padded out the door in his slippers, shading his eyes against the light. He leaned over the back of the couch.

"Are you done yet?" he asked.

Tate sighed. "There's still one book left. Even if I stayed awake all night, I'd never finish." She closed the cover and smoothed it with her hand. "It was fun to read nine stories, though. In fact, this whole weekend has been fun. Scary, too, but exciting."

"You were kind of amazing, Tate," Abner said seriously. "The way you threw us that plank, and then how you saved us in the end."

Tate shrugged. "That was just the magic."

"I don't think so," said Abner. "I had magic in me, too, but I was thinking about things like the speed of the current, and how fast we had to kick against it, and at what angle. Derek had

magic in him, but it all went to his legs—he kicked like a wild man, and it kept turning us around. And Celia had magic in her, but do you know what she did?"

Tate had no idea. "She tried to draw a picture in water?"

"She made up a song about going down the river!" Abner rolled his eyes. "I mean, it was a nice song and all—it had seven verses—but it didn't help us much."

Tate laughed.

Abner wasn't finished. "Sure, maybe the magic helped you think of things to do a little faster than normal. But they were the kind of things you *do* think of. You're the one who comes up with plans when no one else can think of anything."

"That's just thinking ahead," said Tate.

Abner shook his head. "It's being *smart*. It's just not the sort of smart they measure in school."

Tate smiled a little. Maybe Abner was right. But she was still sad that she wasn't going to make the Book Quiz Team.

Abner went back to bed. Tate turned out the

light. She drifted to the window and breathed in the cool September air. The sky shone with stars, and the crescent moon was a little bigger than the night before.

Someone had forgotten to turn off the porch light. It cast long shadows across the grass. There was the big, flat rock, above the wild side of the hill. There was the vegetable garden and the clothesline, too. Her shirt fluttered in the night breeze, light and dry once more. Her jeans flapped lazily, and even her socks blew up and down.

But Mr. Bunny was not swaying in the breeze. He hung straight down, as if he were stuffed with sand instead of cotton, too heavy for the light little breeze to push around.

No, thought Tate suddenly. *Not sand. Water.*

Tate flew down the stairs like a ghost, her nightgown whirling behind her. The grass was cool and damp on her feet as she rounded the vegetable garden. She stubbed her toe on the pumpkin that had grown out as far as the clothesline, but she hardly noticed.

It was as Tate had guessed. Mr. Bunny had stopped dripping, but he was still damp and squishy in the middle. His cotton stuffing had soaked up water like a sponge. His plump rabbit body had been too thick to dry, even after two days on the line.

Gently, carefully, she undid the clothespins that held Mr. Bunny's ears clamped tight. Slowly, cradling the soggy rabbit in her arms, she walked into the house.

She squeezed Mr. Bunny into an empty pitcher. She squished his soft head, and twisted his four legs, and wrung out his long pink ears.

"Sorry, Mr. Bunny," she whispered.

The water was a little fuzzy-looking. She

poured it through a strainer.

Then she put the water into the coffee-maker and pushed the button. She didn't need to add any coffee grounds. All she had to do was heat the water. Her father had said that would make it safe.

Soon steaming-hot water trickled down into a waiting mug. Tate added two ice cubes to cool it down. Then she drank it, every drop. It tasted a little like stuffed rabbit, but that was a small price to pay for magic.

She opened the tenth book and began to read. . . .

The End

About the Author

Lynne Jonell is the author of the popular *Emmy and the Incredible Shrinking Rat*, a *Booklist* Editors' Choice and one of *School Library Journal*'s Best Books of the Year, as well as three more books about the Willow family: *Hamster Magic, Lawn Mower Magic*, and *Grasshopper Magic*. Other works include three children's novels and seven picture books. As for water magic, Lynne likes it splashy, not too cold, and rushing beneath her sailboat!